My Bully, My Friend

Written by Norman Alston
Illustrated by Eric Westray

ISBN: 978-1-734-9439-55 Library of Congress Cataloging-in-Publication Date is available.

Project Specialist/Publisher

Barlow Enterprises, LLC

www. destinystatement. com or text 478-227-5692

Legal Disclaimer

Although the author and publisher have made every effort to ensure that the information in this book was correct at time of press, the author and publisher do not assume and hereby disclaim any liability to any party for any loss, damage, or disruption caused by errors or omissions, whether such errors or omissions result from negligence, accident, or any other cause.

Ordering Information

My Bully My Friend may be purchased in large quantities at a discount for educational, business, or sales promotional use. For more information or to request Mr. Norman Alston as the speaker at your next event email your request to, kingswayintl7@gmail. com

First of all, I give honor and praise to God who allowed this book to come forth. Tiffinnie Alston, my dear wife, you have been by my side for thirty-two, awesome years. This journey that we are on comes straight from God. You are an incredible woman and your passion is amazing. There have been times when I just wanted to quit, but because of who you are and what you understand about God, you never quit on us. Yes! You are the other half of me; you make me whole. Thank you for helping make this book come to life. Your diligence and multiple sacrifices made this happen. Thank you for your prayers when I had no words left. Thank you for always being there for me. Even in the darkest of times, you always saw the light at the end of the tunnel. I love you.

Norm

Acknowledgments

Bringing the dream of my heart to fruition has definitely been a God-journey for the team that helped *My Bully My Friend* come to life. Thank you, Jéneen Barlow, for all that you have done to help us manage and publish this project. Thank you, Kia Johnson, Jackie Young, and Pastor Spencer Rogers for being a friend and for your consistent support. To the awesome group who attended our first book reading, thank you for encouraging my heart with your feedback and kind words. Finally, many thanks to, Barbara Kennedy, Chantel Washington, Doug and Danielle Ruffin, Foster and Nadine Blake, Gerri Matthews, Dr. Robert Carter, Dr. Letitia Price, Audra Marshall, Anthony and Mona Hawkins, and to Milo Atkins who gave us his invaluable "thumbs up." Milo, your approval as a second-grade student was the wind beneath our wings!

My First Day

This is going to be my year, I thought to myself. *I just transferred into a new school. I'll meet new friends and nobody will pick on me anymore.*

I was excited, my clothes were ready, and I was feeling good about myself. I couldn't wait to meet my new friends.

As I lay there in my cozy bed, imagining my perfect year at my new school as I waited for the sun to rise, I could still see the moon brightly shining outside my bedroom window. I kept looking from the window to my clock, waiting for the alarm to go off, but it was taking so long. Finally, I fell back asleep.

Then it happened. There was the sound I had been waiting for all night. The alarm rang.

I jumped out of my bed and started getting ready for my first day at my new school—and for my new friends. My heart was beating fast, and I felt like I could barely breathe.

My mom heard all of the commotion and ran upstairs. "What's the matter? Are you okay?" she asked. "Sit down and calm down for a minute, Al," she insisted.

So I did.

"I have never seen you this happy, honey," my mom whispered as she stared at me with a joyful, perplexed grin. She had no idea how glad I was to leave my old school.

My mom had cooked me a great big breakfast to start the day. She'd fixed eggs, bacon, and my favorite, grits. I finished my breakfast and headed for the car. The time had come for me to meet my new friends.

When we drove up to the front of my new school, I didn't see a lot of kids around. I started to worry and wonder if we were at the right school, because my cousin, who just graduated, said a lot of kids went to this school. He told me I would meet a lot of new friends. So, where were all of my new friends?

As I climbed out of my mom's car, I could hear someone over the loudspeaker saying, "If you are in the fourth, fifth, or sixth grades, report to the gym now." I started to get nervous, because I didn't know where the gym was. As I walked the huge hallways, looking for the gym, I realized I was just going in circles.

Then I heard a sweet voice say, "Are you new here?"

I said, "Who me?"

She started to laugh and said, "Yeah you. What grade are you in?"

Strongly and proudly, I replied, "I'm in the sixth grade."

She said, "Okay, good. Follow me. I'm in the sixth grade, too. We are in Mr. Rome's class."

I followed her and my heart started beating fast, again. I was about to meet my new friends.

When we walked into the classroom, the teacher was standing at the door saying hello to every student who entered. He stopped me at the door and asked me my name.

"My name is Al," I said.

"Hello, Al! Your seat will be on this side," Mr. Rome said as he pointed to my new desk.

I wondered why I was being put on the other side of the room, but quickly found out that I was not the only new student who had transferred into the school.

Alexis, the girl who showed me to our classroom, asked aloud, "Mr. Rome, can Al be my partner?"

He calmly answered, "Okay," then said, "Al, come and take a seat next to Alexis."

Wow, I thought. *I just made my first new friend. Alexis.*

Once everyone was seated, Mr. Rome started to review the classroom rules. I was fine with them because they were just like the rules at my old school. There were a couple new ones, but that didn't bother me at all. Then Mr. Rome began to talk about his summer vacation. There were lots of ooooh's and aaahhh's from us, because of the places he had visited during his summer vacation. He finished sharing and then explained that each student would share something about their summer vacation, too.

I started to get a little nervous, because I was one of the new kids and I didn't want him to call on me first.

Then, to my relief, Mr. Rome said, "Let's save the new students for last."

Student after student went up and talked about what they did during the summer and what they expected their sixth-grade year to be like. There were nineteen kids in our class, and after they all shared, it was my turn. I started out by saying hello to everyone, and then I told them how happy I was to be in a new school this year. I didn't tell them why, because I didn't want them to feel pity for me or laugh at me, and I certainly did not want them to bully me like the people at my old school had done. So, I just spoke and sat down real fast.

After a full day of finding my way through busy hallways and other activities, the bell rang. My first day of school came to an end and I was very happy about how the first day had gone. I didn't get into a fight. I didn't get teased, and I'd made my first new friend, Alexis.

It Keeps Getting Better

When I got up in the morning, I couldn't wait to get to school with my new friends. The first week had gone by so fast! I met new friends, got an A on my spelling and math tests, and the lunch was so good—way better than those lunches from my old school. Even the lunch ladies who worked in the cafeteria were nice. When you came in, they smiled and said, "Good morning" or "Good afternoon," and they gave me a choice of what I wanted to eat for breakfast and lunch.

After lunch, we had one of my favorite classes: gym! I love gym class because I can do everything the teacher asks us to do. I can catch. I can run fast. And I can really shoot the basketball like a pro. I am also a great baseball player. So gym is one of my favorite classes.

Since we were going to play flag football, Mr. James, our gym teacher, let our class choose teams. Everyone got picked to be on a team, and I ended up on Rory's opposing team. Rory was the class athlete. He was strong and he was fast. He was really good at sports and everyone wanted to be on his team.

He's not better than I am, I told myself. But that didn't matter. I knew that as the new kid I would have to take it easy on Rory. I didn't want what happened in my old school to happen again.

We began to play, and because I was the new guy, I had to stick Rory, so we lined up on our side of the ball. The ball was thrown to the gym teacher. Rory took off real fast and ran in front of me, so I knew the gym teacher was going to throw him the ball.

Yup! Just like I thought, he threw the ball to Rory. The ball was right there for me to snatch it and run the other way, but I knew that if I did that, I would lose friends. They would see that I was on the same level as Rory, or better, and that would cause a problem. I didn't need problems, so I jumped up and missed the ball on purpose. It landed right in Rory's hands.

"Touchdown!" yelled the teacher.

The class went wild.

Rory did his touchdown dance, looked at me, and said, "Nice try, partner."

It was okay with me, because they expected Rory to catch the ball, not me. Rory was tall and big, but I was just the normal size. My plan had worked, and everyone was happy – even me.

Well, What Do Ya Know?

School was good, my friends were good, and I was having the best time I'd ever had in school.

We were all in math class one day when Mr. Rome was paged over the loudspeaker. "Mr. Rome," the voice announced. "We will be sending a new student to your class, so keep a look out for him."

"Okay," Mr. Rome responded.

He continued teaching our class, but now we were curious. The class began to chatter.

"I wonder who the new kid is," one of the girls said.

"Yeah, I hope he's cute," the other girls all giggled.

"Me too!" I overheard her friend reply. "We are tired of all of these ugly boys in our class."

They started laughing.

"They are not all ugly," Alexis replied with a smile. "So speak for yourselves, because Al is kind of cute."

I was so embarrassed. "Really?" I yelled out. "Really, Alexis?" I put my hands over my face and my head on my desk. I felt kind of stupid for saying anything.

In the middle of my sulking, the door opened and the new kid walked through the door into my classroom. My eyes got as big as two frisbees when I saw him, and then I got mad. I knew this kid! This was the boy who gave me all of the problems at my old school.

My heart began to beat fast and I could not catch my breath. My head instantly started hurting and my hands became hot and sweaty. I just wanted to leave the classroom as fast as I could. I couldn't believe this was happening to me. I kept saying to myself, *Why here? Why at my new school? Why couldn't you go to another school?*

And then, what do ya know? The only empty seat was next to me.

"Move your books so Jordan can sit down," Mr. Rome said.

I lifted my head and said, "Yes, sir."

Then Jordan recognized me and shouted out, "What's up, Al? I didn't know you went to this school. Yeah, I am definitely going to have some fun with my old buddy, Al."

I raised my hand and said, "Mr. Rome, can I go to the nurse's office? I'm not feeling well."

Mr. Rome said, "Finish taking your test, Al. Then you'll be able to go."

But I just couldn't wait, so I got up and ran out of the class. Mr. Rome yelled for me to come back, and I wanted to listen to him, but I couldn't. My body would not turn around. I ran until I reached the nurse's office.

Alexis got up and came to the nurse's office, where I was sitting and shaking. "Al, what happened? Why did you run out of the class?"

I calmly said, "It's nothing."

She asked me again, "What happened, Al? You can tell me. You just got up and ran out of the class. Mr. Rome was calling you, but you didn't stop."

I lied. "I was not feeling good. My stomach was hurting." I was not telling the truth, but I couldn't let her know that Jordan was my bully at my old school.

Jordan used to take my money and smack me in the face, and he always made the other kids laugh at me. I feared him, but I didn't want anyone to know how I felt. Now, my new school just went from good to bad because of this one person walking through my classroom door.

I couldn't wait for the bell to ring so that I could hurry up and get home. Alexis said she had to get back to class because the bell was getting ready to ring.

"Are you sure you will be okay?" she asked me.

"Yeah," I told her. "I will see you in the morning." Then I yelled, "Thanks for being a good friend!"

She paused, turned around, and said, "It's easy being a good friend to a person like you, Al."

That really made me feel good. No one had ever called me friend. They always called me names and hurt my feelings, but Alexis called me friend and it made me feel so happy that I almost forgot about Jordan.

The bell was about to ring. I was trying to figure out how to leave the nurse's office without anyone seeing me. As soon as the bell rang, I dashed out of the side door. I was fast. No one would ever see me.

It is Friday, so I don't have to see anyone until Monday morning, and I won't see Jordan for a couple of days, I thought to myself. Then I remembered that tomorrow was football tryouts. I had planned to go out for the team, but now, all kinds of thoughts were going through my mind.

My bully, Jordan, would be there, too.

The Day that Changed My Destiny

Saturday, the first day of football tryouts, was really crowded. There were a lot of people trying out because there were so many different teams we could choose to play for. It was not like my old neighborhood. There, we only had one team in our neighborhood league.

I heard the coach say, "Okay everybody, line up so we can do some exercises."

I got in line. The exercises were not bad and I thought I did pretty well.

Then, Coach yelled, "Okay, it's time to see how fast everyone is!"

I knew I could be great at this drill because I was very fast, but I really didn't want everyone to know how fast I was. I decided to come in third place so that no one would be mad at me.

After the race, I heard someone calling my name. I turned around and saw that it was Alexis.

"Hi Al!" she said. "You did really good out there, but I know you could beat all those guys. It looked like you were holding back. You're not running fast as I know you can run."

I started laughing. "Yeah," I said. "I could have, but my leg is hurting and I don't want to hurt myself so I took it easy."

Alexis smiled. "Okay. You still did good, though."

While Alexis and I were talking, Coach called me over to him. "We're going to have a scrimmage soon so that I can see you show-case your skills, Al."

He told everyone to get into one line. Rory ran to get in front of the line. I got behind Rory because I thought the coach would choose every other person to create the teams, and I didn't want to be on Rory's team. I knew that if I were on his team, I would never get the ball. The guys knew him best, so they'd always throw the ball to him, but it turned out that Coach didn't pick the teams the way I thought he was going to pick the teams.

Instead, starting with Rory, who was first in line, he said, "You three guys go there and you three guys go to the other side."

So I ended up on Rory's team anyway, but it wasn't bad. As a matter of fact, he was a way better teammate than I thought he was going to be.

We started to play, and our team was doing really well until one of the boys from the other team got hurt. The coach sent another kid in to take his spot. As the boy who was sent in to replace the kid who had gotten hurt ran over, my eyes got really big.

Oh no, it can't be him, my mind screamed, but as the boy got closer and closer, I knew that he was the one person I did not want to see: Jordan.

I was so scared that I didn't even want to play anymore, but the coach had already blown the whistle. Before Jordan got in the game, I was catching everything. Every ball Rory threw to me, I caught, but now I couldn't catch anything. I was so scared.

Jordan did not help at all. He was talking so much smack to me, and I felt as if he was controlling my mind and my body. Rory started to get mad because he didn't like to lose and definitely wasn't trying to lose to a new guy. That wasn't going to happen.

When we got in the huddle, Rory looked at me, frustrated and confused. "Yo, Al! What's the matter?" he said. "You scared of Jordan or something? Because you haven't caught a ball since he got in the game? Are you okay?"

I heard him, but I didn't say anything.

"Well," Rory said, "he may be able to stop you, but he can't stop me!"

So we switched positions. I became the quarterback and Rory became the receiver.

Rory said, "Okay, this is what we are going to do. I'm going to run a five-yard button hook. Throw the ball to my outside shoulder. When I catch it, you come to the opposite side. I'm going to toss the ball to you so you can score. You got it?" Before I could answer, he said, "Don't be scared. We can do this. Let's show this Jordan boy that he's not all that!"

We did the play just like Rory said, and it worked. Everybody was slapping high fives and hugging.

"Man, you're pretty good!" one of the coaches shouted at me.

Rory ran up to me and said, "I told you he couldn't stop us, Al. That was awesome!"

Jordan was still sitting on the ground. His hands were covering his face, and this time, the crowd wasn't with him. They were laughing at him. I really didn't know how to feel, but I knew that it felt good for people to cheer for me and laugh at Jordan for a change. While I was taking my cleats off, I heard somebody calling my name. It was Alexis.

"Wow, Al! You really are good. That was a great touchdown!" She gave me a big hug, then said, "I'll see you in school on Monday." Then she walked away.

As I was getting the rest of my stuff to leave, Jordan walked over to me and said, "Oh, you think you're funny? That's okay. I'll get you later. You want people to laugh at me? It's on, now. You remember how I had you crying at our old school? This time will be way worse than that, so beware, Touchdown, Al!"

The Tables Are Turning

When I walked into class on Monday, a lot of kids were talking about the weekend's football scrimmage. One by one, they came up to me saying, "Great game, Al!"

One kid said, "Man, why didn't you tell us you were that good?"

I wanted to tell them that I was better than Rory, too, but I kept it to myself because I wanted to keep all my new friends. All of a sudden, it started to get quiet in the classroom. When I lifted my head, I saw that Jordan had entered the room. Everyone got quiet.

Then, out of nowhere, Rory shouted out across the room, "Hey, Jordan, I thought you were good!"

Jordan never answered him.

Then another kid screamed, "Al showed you just how good you are!"

Then another shouted, "Yeah, you can't mess with my man, Al! He's too fast for you."

My stomach tightened up because the kids were teasing and laughing at him about the game. But you know what? I also felt good, because I had people on my side. Now they were doing to

Jordan everything that he had always done to me. I didn't think a day went by that Jordan hadn't made me cry. Now, it was like he and I had traded places. He was the kid who was getting bullied, not me.

I was still scared, though. Jordan said he would make it worse for me than at the old school, so I tried to make sure that I was never by myself. If I saw Jordan, I would always go a different way or talk to somebody while Jordan passed by me. But I knew that avoiding Jordan would not last forever. Eventually, I'd have to confront him face-to-face, and I'll never forget the day I did.

I never went to the bathroom by myself, but Jordan was not in school that day, so I felt safe. I raised my hand and asked Mr. Rome if I could be excused.

"Yes," Mr. Rome said. "But don't be long."

As I was leaving the room, Alexis said, "Hurry up, Al. The test will be starting soon."

Alexis was such a great friend. Because of her help in my classes, I was going to make the honor roll this year, and that was something I had never done at my old school.

"Okay," I replied as I tried to hurry. When I got into the bathroom, there was no one in there but me. While I was washing my hands, I heard the door open, but I never looked up. I just kept washing my hands.

Then I felt a punch to my back. It hurt really bad. I fell onto the floor and felt feet kicking me, and then I heard his voice.

"You thought I would never catch up with you, didn't you? Just my luck, I came to school late today and saw you walking to the bathroom. I warned you that this year would be worse than all the other years."

I began to cry out loud, "Leave me alone, leave me alone, leave me alone!"

Then one of the older boys came into the bathroom and Jordan stopped hitting me and ran into one of the bathroom stalls so no one would see him. I was surprised when the older boy called me by name.

"Al, you okay?" he asked.

"Yes. I'm okay," I responded as I got up off the floor and wiped myself off.

Thankfully, because I was gone so long, Mr. Rome had sent him down to the bathroom to look for me and to make sure that everything was okay. When I went back to the classroom Mr. Rome asked, "What took you so long?"

"Nothing," I replied.

Mr. Rome kept questioning me. "You were in the bathroom that long for nothing? Then tell me why there is a footprint on your back and why your pants are dusty and why you look like you were just in a fight."

"It's okay, Mr. Rome," I responded. "I just slipped on some water that was in the bathroom, but I'll be fine."

He would not stop. "So, Al," he said. "If you slipped in the bathroom, why is there a footprint on your jacket?"

Just then, Jordan walked into class and handed Mr. Rome his late slip. He looked over at me with a smirk on his face, almost daring me to say something about what he just did to me.

I don't know what else to say, I told Mr. Rome, but what I really wanted to say was that it was Jordan's footprint. Instead, I kept saying that I fell because I didn't want any more trouble from Jordan. I wanted to tell Mr. Rome that Jordan beat me up, but I had to keep my cool. I didn't want to get him in trouble, but I was beginning to get very mad. I wanted to get up and punch him in his face, but I knew that if I got in trouble in school, I would have to deal with my father. And my father did not play when it came to getting in trouble in school. I wanted to be like my dad, because he was great and a lot of people loved him. People everywhere said that they wanted to be just like my dad. He was such a great role model for everybody.

What would he say if I got in trouble in school for fighting?

I know he would not be happy with me. Besides, I didn't want that talk from him about how you have to be a role model in this world. I did not want to be reminded that sometimes you have to turn your back on bad situations and be the bigger guy. I could hear that talk coming, and didn't want to have it.

Deep in my heart, I always wondered if my dad knew that I was being bullied. I wanted to fight back, but I didn't want my dad to be judged by people, so I let a lot of things go. My dad's name was respected all over the world. I didn't want to let him down.

He's Really My Friend

The bell rang and we went to our next class. While we were walking into the classroom, Jordan stuck out his foot and tripped me. I fell to the ground and he started to laugh at me. I didn't say anything. I just got up.

Rory came over to me and asked, "Al, what's going on between you and that kid Jordan? Since that boy has come to this school, it's like your whole attitude has changed. When he's around, you're never happy, but when he's not around, you have so much fun. You can tell me what's going on between you two. Did you two have a fight in the bathroom?"

I was quiet. I didn't say anything at all, but Rory would not let it go.

"Come on, Al. Is this boy bothering you? If he is, I'll step to him. You're my boy and I'm not going to let somebody come here and pick on you. We can handle this guy ourselves."

I was in shock. *Wow,* I thought to myself. *The person I thought was against me has turned out to be one of my best friends at this school. He has my back. I really can't believe this. He was the one person I thought*

I would have the most trouble with because we're both athletes and both good. I never thought he would be my best friend.

Rory assured me that he had my back and I didn't have to worry about Jordan bothering me anymore. For years, there had barely been a day when Jordan didn't either say something bad about me or try to harm me in some type of way. It was amazing to be able to walk the hallways and sit in my classes without getting smacked in the head or tripped, and to be able to sit at the lunch table with kids who didn't call me names or knock my tray off the table with all of my lunch on it. This was cool. It was the best.

The one thing Rory didn't see or recognize was that I wasn't scared of Jordan anymore. Actually, I don't think I was ever scared of Jordan; all the people he had on his side made me afraid of him. I was always outnumbered before, but at this new school, Jordan's friends weren't bullies. We both had a lot of the same friends, and they liked both Jordan and me. Out of all of my new friends, Alexis and Rory were my best friends. We were always together, so if you were looking for us all you had to do was call Alexis or Rory's house. I could never invite them to my house because I did not want them to learn my secret.

There was a rumor going around that a professional football player would be coming to visit our school. We had the highest standardized test scores in our city, so our school won a contest for a pro football player to come speak at our school. I never thought that entering that contest was such a great idea for my school, but everyone was so excited about it that I kept my disagreement about it all to myself. I knew that if my school won the contest, my secret would be in trouble. My secret was the one thing I was able to live with as long as no one knew about it. I started to get mad because it was important to me to keep this secret.

When school was over, I raced home, got my cell phone out, and called my dad. "Dad, Dad, Dad!" I yelled into the phone.

Finally, my dad said, "Al, calm down. What is it?"

I was hysterical. "Dad, "I said. "Did you hear that a professional football player is coming to speak at my school next week because we won a contest?"

"Yeah, I just heard about it," my dad said. "But they didn't say who was coming yet. Things like this happen all the time, son. Don't worry, I think your secret is safe."

I was worried, but I said, "I hope you're right, Dad." I still had a big knot in my stomach. I knew that it wouldn't go away until they announced the name of the pro who was coming to my school.

When I got to school the next day, you could tell that whoever the pro player was, spoke about with bullying, because there were a lot of "No bullying" signs going up around our school. One sign said, *Fight Bullying.* Another sign said, *Stand Up to the Bullies,* and *Don't Be Afraid* signs were everywhere. I also saw a pledge that talked about standing up to bullies. The pledge said that people had no right to be bullies, and that **YOU CAN BE A BULLY STOPPER**. The pledge really got to me.

I could become a Bully Stopper, I thought to myself. But first, I had to stop being afraid, myself.

I told myself that when the pro guy came next week, I would talk to him about how to get a bully to leave you alone. Maybe he could give me some pointers on being a Bully Stopper. I started thinking about how I could tell him that Jordan bullied me all the time, and since football was *my* game, I couldn't wait to meet him, anyway.

Now, I was excited about getting to meet the football pro. I couldn't wait to get home to find out who it was going to be. I ran into my house and yelled, "Dad, did you find out who's coming to my school tomorrow to speak?"

He said, "You'll have to find out tomorrow in school, Al."

"Tomorrow? In school? I can't wait until tomorrow, Dad. Tomorrow is coming too slowly."

I wanted my dad to tell me who was coming right now, so that I could have my questions ready. That night, waiting for morning to come was almost as hard as it was for me to wait for the first day at my new school.

Guess Who's Coming

Finally, morning came. When I got to school, they were setting up chairs, lights, and a bunch of other equipment. The camera crew was setting up and the news stations were there, too. The school had hung a large banner in the gym that said, *Bullies, You Lose.*

I was feeling that banner, because that was what I was thinking about Jordan: *You lose. I will no longer allow you to bully me.*

They began to call the students down to the auditorium. The sixth graders waited to hear our names called over the loudspeaker, and finally the secretary said, "Mr. Rome's sixth grade class, please report to the gym."

You could see the joy on everybody's face. Everybody was happy because we were getting ready to meet a professional football player. The boys in our class were going crazy because most of us dreamed of playing professional football one day.

It had been two weeks since we learned that a professional football player would be coming. The teachers and all of my friends were so happy, but for me it was kind of different. Because of my dad's job, I knew a lot of professional players. That was why I was so excited. I could not wait to see who would be coming. Besides, I wanted to talk to them about being bullied. You see, I had been bullied for about three years straight by then.

When I moved to my old school, a lot of the kids didn't like me. It was all over a football game. The new guy, Jordan, who just come to the school, was a good football player, but so was I. Every time we played, he always tried to outshine me on the football field, but I was way better than he was, so he never won. Since he couldn't win on the field, Jordan and his friends began to hit me and call me horrible names each and every day. There wasn't a day that went by that I didn't get smacked, pushed, tripped, or bullied in some way.

I became so sad that I didn't even want to go to school, anymore. They made it really bad for me, just because I was good at sports. I stopped playing because I wanted the hurting to stop, and refused to tell because I thought that telling on them would only make the bullying get worse. What made me the maddest was that all the kids in my school sided with Jordan. They chose to bully me, too. He was the leader, and did everything in his power to make sure that every day was a bad day for me at school. I had no friends. I was all by myself, with no one to talk to. I didn't tell the teachers because I didn't want my dad to look bad. I thought that if he knew his son was afraid of kids at school, he would be more worried about what people would say or think about him rather than about me being bullied. I couldn't take that chance. I couldn't make him look bad. I didn't want to bring shame to him. I loved my dad so much because he gave me everything I wanted, not just everything I needed.

The gym was so crowded, with cameras everywhere. There were so many people on the stage talking. I didn't really care about them; I just wanted to know who the football player was. The lights went out and they begin to show a video. The vide was the highlight film of the person who was going to come out and talk to us. They began to show this player over and over and he was really good, but, in my mind, I kept saying, *No . . . Oh no. It can't be him. It can't be.*

I'd asked my dad did if he knew who the player was, and he didn't tell me because he was the one coming to my school.

I couldn't believe my dad was on the stage and everybody was cheering and shouting his name. It was amazing to see so many people cheering him on. I knew he was good and people loved him, but I didn't know he was loved that much.

The video went off and the lights came up. The people began to scream even louder as my dad walked onto the stage. As he picked up the microphone to speak, Jordan suddenly ran onto the stage and hugged my dad. Tears began running down his face.

Then he started screaming, "It's my favorite player in the whole wide world! You are my hero! Mr. Al Jones, the best safety in football!"

I couldn't believe what I was seeing and hearing. The boy who had been giving me the most trouble and bullying me for years was a fan of my dad. I just couldn't believe it. The principal told Jordan to return to his seat and he did, but not until my dad gave him a hug and a signed football jersey.

I became very angry at my dad and at Jordan. As Jordan sat down, my dad began to speak. He started off by thanking everyone for coming and having him here to speak about bullying. He told the audience that bullying was something that we needed to stop and stop quickly, because it did nothing but hurt good people.

Then he said he wanted to thank someone who was very special to him.

"He's my son and he goes to this school," my dad said. "He asked me if I knew who was coming to speak. I told him that I didn't know, but now I'm here. I know he's saying, 'Dad, why didn't you tell me it was you who was going to speak?' But I didn't know until this morning when I went to practice. My coach told me that I had a very special place to speak this morning. So, when I found out that I was speaking at my son's school, I was very happy, because I was going to be able to speak at my little hero's school about bullying. You might ask why I call him a hero. I call my son a hero because he never gets into trouble. He's never given me any reason to be upset with him. He always tells me how great I played in my games and he always supports me. We have moved so many times, but he never complained. I'm not always home, because of my games and because I talk about bullying all over the country." Then he said, "Help me welcome the best kid in the world, and my young hero, my son, Al, to the stage. Al, come and share the stage with your father."

When I got up to go to the stage, people were amazed that my dad was a pro player and I hadn't told anyone. People were clapping loudly and it felt incredible to be standing up there with my dad. He talked about bullying, but I never told him that, for the last three years, I had been a victim of bullying. After today, I had to tell him.

What a day! I got to spend time with my dad as the guest professional football player on the stage at my new school.

After leaving the gym, we returned to our classes and people wanted to know all about how it felt to be a professional football player's son.

Alexis said, "Al, I knew there was something you were hiding. I just didn't know what it was. That's why you act like you do, that's amazing. You have everything, but you don't let it go to your head. I'm really glad to be your friend now."

Rory said, "Yes, Alexis, I know what you mean. This guy is good in sports, but no wonder, look at his dad! And he's still humble. I know he's very good, I can feel it when we play. He's fast and he catches everything. But my question is: Why do you let people beat you when you know you can beat them? And the biggest question is: Why do you allow people to bully you and never speak up?"

I began to explain myself, but Jordan's phone rang. "Mr. Rome, can I answer this? It's my dad." Jordan began to talk to his dad on the phone.

The next thing we all heard was a siren-like scream. Jordan fell on the ground and began to cry. Mr. Rome ran over to ask Jordan what was wrong.

Crying hard, Jordan looked up through his tears and said, "Mr. Rome, my mom just died."

All of our classmates got up, put their arms around Jordan, and told him it was going to be okay. "We have your back, Jordan," the class said.

I came over and put my arms around Jordan, too. I truly understood what he was going through, because I'd lost my mom at a young age, too. If it had not been for my stepmom, I don't know how I would have made it through.

No More Secrets

When I got home, my dad was there.

"Thanks for coming to the school today, Dad," I said. "I learned something new." I also told him my secret about being bullied for the last three years.

He asked me why I hadn't said anything to him. I told him I didn't want to cause any trouble for him as a pro football player. He told me that I was the most important person in his life, and that football did not come before his being a father to me. He told me that the reason he'd gotten involved with the anti-bullying team was because he never wanted his son to be bullied. I told him all about Jordan and what he had been doing to me all these years. Just as my dad started to tell me again that sports did not come before my safety, the doorbell rang.

I opened my door to find that my classmates, including Alexis, Rory, and even Jordan had come to visit me. What a surprise! Jordan was at my house.

I let all them in.

Jordan had come to say sorry for bullying me. He told me that he wanted to be my friend, because I was different from anybody he'd ever known.

"Why would you come and hug somebody who bullied you every day?" he asked me. Before I could answer him, he explained that he also wanted to be friends with me because I didn't let what he did to me stop me from hugging him when he was feeling the worst he had ever felt in his life. He said that he was glad he'd come to this school because it changed him from a bully into a friend.

Jordan also thanked me for allowing him to meet his hero, my dad, who was his favorite football player. He quoted some of the things my dad was saying on the stage and then said he wanted to be like me. He explained that he wanted to help people instead of bully them. Then he thanked me again for being a real friend.

"At our old school, people didn't stop me from harming others. They just joined in. I thought I was cool and that I could do anything I wanted to do, but you showed me what being a friend really is. Even though I did not deserve it, you didn't turn your back on me in my time of need. You put me first, despite your feelings."

I appreciated everything he said. My dad was right: You have to be the bigger guy. Always.

A lot went wrong, but so many great things happened, too. Because my dad was a spokesperson for anti-bullying, we decided to have an anti-bullying team at our school as well. We had t-shirts, hats, and our very own saying: #BulliesYouLose!

Through a very tough situation, Alexis, Jordan, Rory, and I became the best of friends.

About the Author

Norman and Tiffinnie Alston were both born and raised in Camden, NJ. Their mission is to empower people for purpose and they are especially gifted when it comes to educating and empowering youth.

They believe, when you know where you've been and know who you are, you can achieve greatness. This is why they founded Kings Way International (KWI) Inc. and wrote, directed, and produced the stage play, "Why Bully Me?"

Norman has worked with youth for over 40 years. As a former police officer, youth advocate, coach of multiple sports for several leagues, and a valued staff person in his local school system, he has seen his share of bullying. In fact, as a young boy, Norman was bullied, but he learned to stand up for himself. That experience drove him to ensure that no other child would be treated unfairly in sports or in life. It is also what led Norman to become a police officer and what inspired his wife, Tiffinnie and him, to become ministers.

Norman is trained in conflict and gang resolution, as well as, in working with children who have developmental issues. His training and experience enable him to hear and understand issues from the child's perspective.

The song "Be a Father," written by Tiffinnie, speaks to the need for a positive relationship between a father and son. Healthy father-son relationships are key within the family dynamic and research shows that fathers and positive male role models in general are effective advocates when it comes to doing the work needed to stop children from being bullied.

Mentoring, helping people, and healing the family are core components of KWI and this is evident based upon the types of plays and programs they develop. *My Bully, My Friend* is their most recent project and the Alstons wholeheartedly believe that many more children will be saved from the tragic effects of bullying as people read and share this beautiful story of how one boy's bully becomes his good friend.

Made in the USA
Middletown, DE
16 January 2021